THE JUNIOR NOVEL

With thanks to Dr. David

*Based on the motion picture screenplay
written by James Schamus*

First published in the USA by HarperCollins*Publishers* Inc. in 2003
First published in Great Britain by HarperCollins*Entertainment* in 2003

HarperCollins*Entertainment* is an imprint of HarperCollins*Publishers* Ltd,
77 - 85 Fulham Palace Road, Hammersmith, London W6 8JB

The HarperCollins website address is
www.fireandwater.com

1 3 5 7 9 10 8 6 4 2

ISBN 0 00 716242 1

Printed and bound in Great Britain by Clays Ltd, St Ives plc

www.thehulk.com

HULK™

THE JUNIOR NOVEL

Based on the Diaries
of Bruce Banner

HarperCollinsEntertainment
An Imprint of HarperCollinsPublishers

TO: OUR READERS
FROM: THE EDITORS

We have always dedicated ourselves to maintaining a strict level of discretion and high quality in the subject matter that our publications explore. To that end, we do not participate in the publishing of "sensationalistic" works designed to capitalize on public tragedies and disasters.

Because of these demanding standards, we initially had no intention of publishing any books covering what many have described as "the story of the century." We are referring, of course, to the monstrous creature that the media and the general public have come to know as "the Hulk."

However, we were forced to reconsider our position upon receiving "the diary." We were neither looking for, nor expecting it.

How was the diary acquired? Quite simply: One day a package arrived at the desk of one of our editors. In the carefully wrapped package we found the diary—or, more correctly, a series of diaries—personal journals, all handwritten, covering a period of close to twenty years. We were astounded to discover that none other than Bruce Banner himself kept these journals . . . Bruce Banner, also known as the Hulk.

The diaries go back to the days when Banner was a teenager, when he was known as Bruce Krenzler, having taken the name of his adoptive mother, Marion Krenzler.

Young Bruce had no idea of his true identity at that time; no idea where he really came from, or of the strange things that had been done to him. It had all happened when he was much too young to remember.

In these diaries, we see Bruce slowly start to comprehend, over a period of years, that he is not like other people; that he is capable of doing strange and even terrible things.

We realized that this was a view of Bruce Banner and his tortured alter ego, the Hulk, which went beyond the simplified portrayal of the single most destructive creature of modern times. These diaries enabled us to see the human side of the Hulk. We came to realize that those who call him a monster do not comprehend the full scope of the tragedy that is the life of Bruce Banner.

We have no idea where these diaries came from. We have some suspicions. But we do not and cannot know for sure, and so it would not be appropriate for us to speculate. We have, however, had three different handwriting experts review the diaries, and they have all said the same thing: They are absolutely genuine.

What you are about to read are selections from the actual diaries of Bruce Banner. We could have simply reprinted every page, but there are far too many. Some are filled with such mundane entries as, "Picked up my clothes from the dry cleaners today. They got the mustard out."

Instead you will find published here the sections

that are most relevant to the story of one man with a bizarre secret that—in the beginning—even he did not fully understand. These diary excerpts will give you the most complete picture that anyone has ever been given of the Hulk.

And, if nothing else, they remind us that no one should ever be judged solely by what appears on the surface . . . even if that surface is bright green.

April 18, 1983

I had another one of those weird dreams. It's what Mom calls "recurring" dreams. I have them over and over again, no matter how much I wish they'd just go away.

In the dream, I see myself as a little boy, which is pretty strange since when I'm awake, I don't have *any* memory of my childhood. I hear voices. I think they're supposed to be my biological mother and father. In real life, I wouldn't know my parents if I fell over them, but in the dream, I know it's them.

They're arguing about something. I sense they're always arguing. I'm playing with two floppy stuffed animals. Mom and Dad are yelling louder and louder, and suddenly the two dolls just sort of . . . change. It's like they're changing into two monsters, fighting with each other. They leap out of my hands, hitting each other all by themselves, and then suddenly I hear a scream. . . .

Well, that was my dream, anyway.

In reality, the only scream came from me when I woke up. It took me a minute to realize I was in my own bedroom. Mom called my name, and that helped pull me out of it.

She flipped on the light and I squinted, rubbing sleep out of my eyes. I was shaking. It was kind of embarrassing. I'm fourteen years old, but I was as scared as any little kid waking from a bad dream.

"Another nightmare, Bruce?" she asked.

I may not remember my real mom, but my adoptive mom couldn't be any more loving to me. I didn't want to worry her. I know you should never lie to your parents, but I lied to Marion Krenzler just the same. "I don't know," I said. "I don't remember."

She came over to me and held me until the shaking stopped. I'm still sorry I lied. But why should I get her upset over things even I don't completely understand?

February 27, 1986

As if senior year weren't stressful enough, something really strange happened in school today. And for some reason, I feel as though something like it occurred a long time ago . . . but I can't remember when.

I was in the school lab, working with a microscope and studying some cell samples.

And then Alice came over.

Alice—she's never noticed me before. She's never cared about me at all. Why should she? I'm a skinny guy, no muscles, not on any sports teams or any-

12

thing. My hair is brown and shapeless and kind of hangs down. My ears stick out, my nose is weird. I'm really nothing special. But Alice, she's beautiful. And now she was making time for me.

So there I was, looking in the 'scope, and then I smelled her perfume, and she was right next to me.

"Hi Bruce. What are you doing?" she asked.

I tried to keep it together. Even so, my voice was trembling as I said, "It's cool. Uh . . . you can check out the DNA, you know." I wanted to explain that DNA, of course, makes up the "building blocks" of humans. It's like the blueprint inside you that decides whether you'll be short or tall, blue- or brown-eyed, and a million other things.

"Can I see?" she asked.

So I said sure, and she leaned in close over the microscope. She smelled like flowers and the outdoors, and she said, "You know, I really get turned on by brainy guys."

I could hardly stand, my legs were shaking just from her being so close, and I stepped back. The next thing I knew I was stumbling over a stool behind me. I hit the floor while the metal stool clattered away, and suddenly I heard people laughing.

I twisted around on the floor and looked behind me, and there were *all these kids*, all grouped at the door and pointing and laughing. And worst of all was Alice, she was laughing the loudest, and she said, "Poor Bruce, you are such a nerd!"

It was a setup. All of it, a big setup, to make me look stupid.

I got so mad. And I don't get mad. I never do. I'm not sure why. I've always just believed deep down that getting mad is the worst thing I can possibly do. It's like I've always known it, but never exactly known why.

I found out.

Because the angrier I got, the more my body started to shake, like I was having some sort of seizure. My back started to twist, my shoulders felt like they were bending outward. I looked at my arms and there were some sort of . . . of weird bumps, like . . . like there were alien creatures running around under my skin.

I grabbed the side of the table and tried to haul myself up. Everyone was still laughing. They didn't see what was happening, didn't see any of it.

I fell forward onto the table, scattering everything. There was a lit Bunsen burner there, and I knocked that over, too. A tube of chemicals over-turned, and they instantly ignited. Just like that, the whole table was on fire.

Everyone ran. Everyone except me. My whole body hurt too much. And then the overhead sprin-klers came on, soaking the lab, and the cold water washed over me and helped me calm down. I looked at my arms. They were normal.

But at that point I realized I'm anything *but* normal.

I have some sort of, I don't know, allergic reaction to getting angry. I don't know why. But I do know that I have to keep calm from now on, because if I don't, something will happen.

Something terrible.

August 27, 1986

Mom looked so sad today, I almost wish I wasn't getting ready to go off to college.

It's an exciting opportunity, I know. I have so much to learn, and I also have a lot to contribute. Some of the top minds in the country teach at the California Institute of Technology. Still . . . I will miss Mom.

I didn't realize quite how much I would miss her until I was sitting in my room today, surrounded by stacks and stacks of books. I knew I couldn't bring all of them with me to the dorm. I never dreamed it would be so hard to choose which ones to take. As I was sitting there, trying to get it all sorted out, Mom came in. She didn't say anything to me about keeping my room straightened up. In fact, she looked at the mess almost as if she were going to miss having it around.

She leaned against the door and folded her arms, like she was waiting for me to say something. "Hey, Mom," I said.

She sighed and said, "Bruce." I'd never heard my name sound so wistful before. "Already off to college. I'm going to miss you, terribly." She walked over to me and ran her fingers through my hair, mussing it up. "But someday you will be a remarkable scientist."

"Like my father?" I asked.

Her fingers tightened a little in my hair. She wasn't meaning to pull on it or anything, but she tugged at the roots nevertheless. I jumped a little and I think she realized, because immediately she let go and ran her hands along her apron. She was smiling in a pained kind of way. As if I'd brought up things she really, really didn't want to think about.

"Do you remember him?" she asked.

17

"No," I admitted. "But you said once, he was a scientist."

She looked confused, and walked to the far side of the room. "Did I?" she said, and it almost seemed as if she was ready to deny having said it. I have no idea why she would. Then she forced a sickly sort of smile and continued, "I must have been guessing, seeing how brilliant you are."

Then, whatever was going through her mind, it must have passed because she smiled one of her more normal smiles and said, "Please. Come here."

So I stood up and walked over to her. She draped her arms around my shoulders and put her forehead against mine, the way she used to do when I was younger and upset about something. "Someday," she said, "you will discover that there is something inside you . . . so special . . . some kind of greatness, I am sure. Someday you will share it with the whole world."

Mom always knows just what to say. Still, I can't help but wonder. Just because you have something in you, something special, that's not always a good thing. If Mom's right, then whatever I've got . . .

Is it a good thing? Or a bad thing?

I guess I'll find out.

18

June 18, 2001

What an incredible day this has been.

I began work today at the Lawrence Berkeley lab in Berkeley, California. Dr. Lawrence, who runs the place, was very impressed with my track record. He said the lab first noticed me back in my college days. Professors were recommending me to scouts from the lab because of my advanced work. Now that I've had a few years of "seasoning" (that's what he called it), they thought I was ready to come aboard. I'm barely into my 30s, and I'm working in one of the most important labs in the country.

Can it get any better than that? Well, yes, possibly.

Because I also met this lovely woman at the lab. She's working on a fascinating project involving nanotechnology. "Nanomeds," she calls them—the microscopic creatures that are inhaled and, once they're under the skin, can instantly repair any damage to the human body. It would become literally impossible for people to die from injuries.

Plus, her research goes together perfectly with my studies of speeding up the growth of cells.

The other thing is—she's beautiful. Smart and beautiful, and I'm kind of sure she likes me. Her name is Dr. Elizabeth Ross, but she said I should call her Betty. Betty Ross. It's a very nice name, and she's a very nice person.

I think she's interested in going out with me. But since we work together, it probably wouldn't be a good idea for us to start any sort of personal relationship.

July 4, 2001

Betty and I have had our fourth date in two weeks. We went to a fireworks display in San Francisco to celebrate Independence Day.

I looked back on my entry from a couple of weeks ago, in which I said I shouldn't date Betty. Ah, well. I guess anyone and anything can change. Even me.

Still . . . sometimes I have trouble being comfortable around her. I almost feel as if . . . someone else is watching her. Watching me. Watching us. Even when there's no one else around, it's like we're never quite alone. If I didn't know better, I'd say the someone else is in my own head, staring at the two of us without saying a word. Just . . . growling somehow, like a caged animal.

Sometimes I think I'm going a little crazy.

Well, maybe this is what being in love is like.

September 23, 2002

Betty and I have been together for over a year. We went up to her cabin in the woods this weekend, as we've been planning for ages. But it didn't go very well at all.

The trip started off fine. But then Betty started acting very distracted. I asked her what was bothering her, and she told me she'd been having bad dreams. Terrible dreams.

I told her to do what I do—don't sleep. She thought I was kidding. I wasn't, of course. The dreams I used to have as a teenager, they've only gotten worse as I've grown up. I hardly sleep at all anymore. But I didn't tell her that.

Betty told me about her dream. She thinks it has something to do with when she was a little girl, growing up in an army installation called Desert Base. Turns out her father is a general in the army: Thaddeus Ross, although apparently he's called "Thunderbolt" because of his temper.

In her dreams, she and her father are playing, and suddenly the sky gets dark, and in the distance some sort of bomb goes off. Then she sees a young boy in the window of a house. Little Betty is crying, and then a hand covers her mouth—and this is the most disturbing part—it's my hand covering her mouth.

I told her I would never hurt her. And she looked at me and said, "You already have."

"How?" I said.

"You're breaking my heart," she told me.

I knew what was bothering her. She says I'm "too tightly wrapped." That I never show my full emotions. I never get angry or happy or anything. I'm always calm, even-tempered Bruce. She says I'm hiding things from her.

24

Maybe she's right. Sometimes I think I'm hiding things from myself.

I didn't tell her that. Instead I told her that if she feels that way, we should stop dating. We should just work together instead. I didn't mean it, though. I didn't want to stop dating her.

But she thought it over and said she thought I was right. So . . . that's that.

I guess I should be happy. We weren't going to work out as a couple. Better to end it before it goes too far.

Just be there for the work.

That's all that's important.

The work.

25

March 15, 2003

Stared at myself for a long time in the mirror while I was shaving today.

Weirdest thing.

I know what my eyes look like. Everyone knows what their eyes look like.

So why did I feel like somebody else's eyes were staring back at me from the mirror? Someone I sort of knew, but didn't really.

I need to start getting some sleep. This is ridiculous.

The gammasphere is ready for testing. It's amazing to have this room specially built for our experiments. It's completely sealed off from the rest of the lab. We can't take chances with gamma rays.

We're using gamma rays for our experiments because they have many of the same uses as X rays, especially in the treatment of cancer (which, of course, we're hoping our work will cure!). However, even though gamma rays are just particles of light—tiny and invisible—they're still dangerous enough to make you sick, or even kill you, if too much radiation from the gamma rays hits your body. It would be like getting the worst sunburn of your life, inside *and* out. But we have enough safety measures in place to prevent accidents.

The process couldn't be simpler. We take a test animal—a frog, to start with—and have it inhale the nanomeds.

Then we use a gamma-particle gun to damage the frog—nothing huge. We make cuts and small burns to start out; very controlled use of gamma rays, as I said. If the nanomeds can repair radiation damage, they can repair anything.

We may be standing before the dawn of a new era in human medicine.

27

March 16, 2003

First test of the gammasphere.

Frog blew up.

Wasn't pleasant. I thought my assistant, Ned Harper, was going to cry. He really liked that frog. He shouldn't get attached to things, especially to lab animals.

The only thing I've learned from the experiment is that a frog makes a very bizarre croaking sound before it explodes. That's interesting, but not of much help to the project . . . or, for that matter, to the frog.

Hopefully things will go better tomorrow.

Spent the past week blowing up frogs. Somehow when I was going to school, I didn't see this as part of my future—helping to clean up frog guts for a week. This afternoon we ran out of frogs. Further tests delayed until more frogs can be obtained.

I don't know whether to be annoyed by the fact that we're out of frogs or relieved. One thing I know for certain: I'm getting tired of seeing frog skin all over the place. Frankly, if I never see green skin again, it will be too soon.

April 1, 2003

We had to make a presentation today to the board of directors of the laboratory. I was hoping to give them good news. Unfortunately, we didn't have any. Our latest test frog, "Freddie," met the same unpleasant end as all those who went before him.

We came so close to success, too. When the gamma rays struck Freddie across his belly, they left a one-inch cut in him that healed almost immediately. The nanomeds were working, and then— *blam!* No more frog.

It's a shame nanomeds can't heal a broken heart

as well. Betty came by my office today. She seemed so sad. I'm not sure why she's being this way. *She's* the one who broke off our relationship, because I couldn't "express" myself enough. But today she told me, "I'm just having a hard time, us being apart, but still seeing you every day, working together . . . it makes me feel more lonely than ever." Then she shrugged and said, "But what can you do?"

I told her I could still appreciate and admire her as a friend. It didn't seem enough for her. It's frustrating.

The nanomeds are even more frustrating. Right now, our nanomedical "cures" have been more deadly than the diseases they would treat. They attack injuries and infections really violently; they're like an army that's so determined to destroy an enemy, they're willing to nuke an entire city to do it, without caring about the damage to innocent people. All they care about are their instructions to destroy. Maybe they remember their instructions too well.

In some ways, people can be like that, too. Perhaps, to stay in balance, and alive, we must forget as much as we remember.

Met someone today I'd rather not have met.

His name is Glen Talbot. He "used to be" quite a few things. He used to be in the army. He used to serve with Betty's father, the General.

And he used to be Betty's boyfriend.

Now it turns out he works for a company called Atheon. It's a huge, nationwide research organization, and one of the things it loves to do is buy out smaller labs and snap up all their assets. It also has major ties to the military.

The last thing we need is for Atheon to get its

hands on this lab and our work. We're developing the nanomeds to find ways to cure sick or injured people. But Atheon would probably take the research and try to find ways to turn it into a weapon. I talked to Betty about it, and what she told me only confirmed my worries.

According to Betty, Talbot told her, "I've been hearing interesting things about what you guys are doing here. This could have some significant applications."

That word "significant" is very . . . well . . . significant.

April 3, 2003

Something very odd happened tonight.

I had just had another discussion with Betty about Talbot. He has offered jobs at Atheon to both Betty and me. I don't want to have anything to do with that company, but Betty actually seemed to be considering it. She came to my office and said, "Glen may be a jerk, but you may want to think about it. More resources and equipment. Less red tape."

I told her I wasn't interested. I just want to focus on my work. I think she understood, although she did tell me she wished I'd show the slightest hint of jealousy over Talbot's coming back into her life.

What would be the point of letting my emotions get the better of me? I simply don't understand. People call jealousy the green-eyed monster. Is that what Betty wants from me? To become a green-eyed monster? As if I'd let *that* happen.

That wasn't the strange thing, though.

After Betty said good night, I heard her chatting with someone just outside my door. I'm pretty sure it was the janitor, considering I heard the squeaking wheels of his clean-up cart. Then he pushed his cart along, and Betty left, and I was alone in the building. At least I thought I was.

But when I was leaving for the night, I came across this mangy-looking poodle sitting in the middle of the hallway, alone. I went toward it to pet it, saying, "Hey there, who are you?"

The next thing I knew, it was baring its teeth at me, if you can call them teeth. They were all rotting away, and the dog had this demented look in its eyes.

I backed up and looked around to see if the thing's owner was anywhere in sight. I thought maybe it belonged to the janitor. But there was nobody around. It started to follow me, still growling. I got out as quickly as I could, worried it would run after me, and sink its teeth into my leg. It might have rabies or who knows what diseases?

When I got outside the lab, there was a security guard on his way in. A big bruiser of a man. I said, "Hey! There's a poodle in there!"

Of course he looked at me as if I were some sort of idiot. "A poodle. Sure. Yeah, we'll look into it," he said, talking to me as he would to a child.

I headed home as quickly as I could. I don't know why, but I felt as if I had just managed to avoid something. Something . . . awful. And I don't even know what it was.

April 4, 2003

Even though I'm dating this entry April 4, it still feels like April 3rd because it's 2:27 in the morning and I haven't managed to sleep one bit since I got home.

I worked and worked on all manner of figures, calculations, sketches, and DNA sequences. I've tried and tried to figure out what's been going wrong with the nanomeds research.

Nothing. No luck. So I've started making another entry in this journal. Maybe that will clear my head.

I'm sitting at the window of my bedroom, staring

out at a willow tree. Its long, dangling branches look like an intricate, dancing web. They're starting to look like . . . they remind me of those toys, the stuffed animals I've dreamed about, fighting. . . .

It's crazy.

Then again, maybe I'm crazy.

Some man just walked past, and he stopped and looked up at me. He probably thinks I'm crazy, too.

Need some sleep. Have to try to get even a couple of hours. Will stop writing now.

It's 4:48 in the morning. I fell asleep sitting up. Had those dreams again—the toys crashing together, and a man and woman yelling. A baby opening his mouth and screaming, and it sounded like a primal scream.

I woke up. And outside . . .

That man. That man is still there. Just standing there, looking as if he's wearing the shadows that surround him. And there are three dogs with him. They all look as if they need to see a vet. Poorly fed, ungroomed. One seems to be some sort of mastiff . . . and there's a pit bull . . . and . . . that poodle? Is that the poodle? The one from the lab?

I slam shut the blinds, trying to block it out. Take some breaths. Take it easy. Look back out, and if he's still there, call the poli—

He's gone.

Gone.

Maybe I imagined him. Maybe I'm thinking . . .

I don't know what I'm thinking anymore. I feel as if the line between fantasy and reality is sliding, blurring, and the incredible is becoming more and more possible.

Sleep. Please, sleep . . .

April 5, 2003

I reread yesterday's entries. It's almost embarrassing—seeing that stream-of-consciousness narrative. It's almost as if it were written by another person entirely. Could I really have been that confused, frightened? It's amazing what the mind can do to you, the tricks it can play. How you can make yourself almost crazy with worry. Especially when deprived of sleep.

Just think what I'd be like if I did what Betty asked. If I let myself be more emotional. I'd be out of control. What a truly horrifying thought.

April 8, 2003

Glen Talbot continues to hover around the lab. I got there and, first thing, he was chatting with Betty as if he had a right to be there . . . or even had a right to her. I could see the way he was looking at her. It's none of my business, and yet I found it extremely irritating.

He came over to me as if we were associates or even friends, and said, "You know, Dr. Krenzler, we've never had the chance to get to know each other properly."

The way he said my name—"Dr. Krenzler"—as if

41

it sounded foolish. As if it isn't even my name. But I certainly wasn't going to let him get to me.

I said, "That's because I don't want to get to know you, properly or improperly," and added, "Leave." Not even "please leave." Just "leave." Betty tried to calm me, but I said, "*Now,*" so he knew I meant business.

He smiled indifferently and said, "No worries."

But then he came closer to me, speaking so softly that Betty couldn't hear him, and said, "But let me give you a little heads up: There's a thin line between friendly offer and hostile takeover. I've done my homework. The stuff you're doing here is dynamite. Think: Soldiers imbedded with technology that makes them instantly repairable on the battlefield, in our sole possession. That's a heck of a business."

I had been right. All he wanted was to take our developments and make them into tools of the military. "That's not what we're doing here," I told him. "We're doing this science for everyone."

Talbot shook his head and looked at me with pity. "You know, someday I'm going to write a book. I'm gonna call it *When Stupid Ideals Happen to Smart,*

Penniless Scientists. In the meantime, Bruce, you'll be hearing from me." And out of my lab he swaggered.

I'm not sure how things could possibly get any worse.

April 9, 2003

I have to remind myself never to write such things as "how could things possibly get any worse?"

I should be dead.

According to everyone I've spoken to in the past hour, by all logical means of measurement, there is simply no way I can still be alive and writing this. Yet, as my mother always said, here we are.

The accident . . . the accident in the lab. My memory of it is a blur. Everything happened so fast. As best as I can recall, this is what happened:

We were getting ready to use the gammasphere on another test subject. We were going to double the exposure of the nanomeds on the frog, although that seemed fairly drastic. But we were running out of possible ways to make the procedure work and, frankly, we were running low on frogs again, so the feeling was that we didn't have that much to lose.

Harper was readying the gammasphere. Betty was talking to me about my favorite subject, Glen Talbot—again—while Harper was busy fixing a problem with the interlock switch that seals the door to the gammasphere. As was standard procedure, he was wearing a breathing mask so as not to accidentally inhale any free-floating nanomeds.

Betty was busy telling me that she could talk to her father about putting pressure on Talbot to get him out of our hair. This was quite a gesture on Betty's part, considering she hasn't spoken to her father in years.

At that moment, Harper asked me to come out and take a look at the circuit, saying it seemed "kind of fried." I went out there immediately because, of course, if the interlock wasn't working, we would all be "kind of fried." Without the interlock operating correctly, the entire lab facility would be flooded with gamma radiation the moment we fired the gamma canisters.

The automatic countdown for the discharge of the canisters had begun, but I wasn't worried; I figured those could be shut down at any time. Just as I reached the gammasphere, the interlock circuits began to spark. Harper tried to back out, but his breathing mask was caught on the equipment.

I ran and yanked his mask clear of the snag. I heard the countdown continuing and wondered why it kept going with both of us still exposed to the sphere. I didn't realize the short circuit had blown out the backup systems. Betty was hammering away on the keyboard at my workstation. It wasn't responding. The nanomeds and gamma canisters were about to release. There was no way to halt the countdown, and the interlock was still open.

I heard the hiss of the nanomeds being released, and the gamma canisters were about to fire. The test frog, sitting on his platform, croaked at me. The frog wouldn't be the only thing croaking in a minute.

I had no choice. I threw myself directly in front of the gamma canisters just as they began to fire.

I heard later on that people said I was heroic. I didn't think of it as heroic. Just desperate. All I knew was that if I didn't do something, Betty was going to die, Harper was going to die. Good, innocent people were going to die. I didn't think about my own likely death. I just thought about preventing theirs. I don't know if that's heroism or just short-sightedness.

Witnesses said my body glowed green from the radiation. I felt warmth flooding through me, and I heard screams and the sounds of alarms. The next thing I knew, I was on my knees, my mind whirling. I wasn't thinking about the gamma radiation, or my likely death, or even Betty, who was apparently screaming my name at the top of her lungs.

Instead I was seeing those toys, those shape-changing stuffed animals from my dreams, spinning around in my head, and the bright detonation of a bomb in a faraway desert. Then everything went black.

Well . . . greenish black.

The next thing I heard was the low muttering of voices. No alarm. No shouting. The voices sounded astonished, filled with disbelief. I opened my eyes and sat up, and there were startled gasps from nearby people. I looked around and realized I was in the lab's infirmary. The place was packed with doctors and nurses, and I was hooked up to monitors, with intravenous solutions being pumped through tubes stuck in my arms.

They were all looking at me as if I'd grown a third eye in the middle of my forehead.

They told me I'd been unconscious for about two hours.

Other than that, I was fine.

They allowed Betty to come in and see me while they took my blood pressure for what seemed like the tenth time. I told her I'd absorbed barely enough radiation for a slight tan, even though the doctors were claiming I should have looked like burnt toast. Except obviously I didn't, so I think it was pretty clear who was right and who was wrong.

It was Betty, literally shaking with relief, who brought up an interesting theory. She said, "The radiation was bad enough. What I'm talking about are the nanomeds. How could you survive it?"

"Wait. You're saying I was exposed to the radiation, but that the nanomeds repaired me?" I asked. "Come on, Betty."

"I don't have any other explanation," she said.

I thought about it, and it was truly an exciting prospect. "But . . . if it's true, then . . . they worked. They actually worked."

She immediately disagreed. "We haven't come close to controlling them. You know that. They would have killed anyone else. Bruce, maybe there's something . . . *different* in you."

That gave me a lot to think about. And I was going to have plenty of time to think, because they wanted to keep me under observation in the infirmary for twenty-four hours.

49

April 10, 2003

I'm writing this in the middle of the night, in the infirmary. My head is whirling. My mouth is dry. I don't know what to think, except that maybe I'm losing my mind completely.

I was lying in bed, trying to sleep despite the steady drone of the monitors. Illumination from the streetlights was filtered through the window, giving things such a dreamlike quality that, even now, it's hard to believe what I witnessed was real.

The sound of dogs woke me, soft growls coming

from their chests and sounding like jet engines. They were five feet away from me, sitting around a man, and I recognized him as the man who'd been standing outside my house a few nights ago.

He was wearing a janitor's uniform. He worked at the lab. I suddenly wondered if he was the guy whom I'd overheard Betty speaking with the other night. Was he following me? Stalking me? What in the world was going on?

He just sat there, staring at me. And suddenly he said, "Your name is not Krenzler. It's Banner."

"What?" I said. I could barely process that he was even there, much less what he was talking about.

"Your name. It's Banner. Bruce Banner." More softly, he added, "Bruce."

And then he told me, he . . . he said he was my father.

Well, of course, I told him that couldn't be. That my parents died when I was a small boy.

Instead he got this bizarre "conspiracy theory" look on his face and said, "That's what they wanted you to believe. The experiments, the accident—they

51

were top secret. They put me away for thirty years—away from you, away from our work. But they couldn't keep me forever. After all, I'm sane. They had to admit it."

I didn't know who "they" were, but whoever thought this . . . this lunatic dog-man was "sane" should have his own sanity checked.

I told him he was crazy, that he should leave at once. The old man scowled, and the dogs growled at me. It was as if they could sense his moods and were ready to act on them. He told them to heel, and they backed off.

He stood and said, "We're going to have to watch that temper of yours."

He walked out, the dogs following him, their long nails click-clacking on the tiled floor.

I ran out after them, although truthfully I have no idea why. I should have just been grateful to see him go. Instead I pursued him into the hallway. But he was gone.

The nurse was dozing at her station, and I woke her up.

"Where did he go?" I asked.

She looked at me as if I were the crazy one, and said, "Who do you mean?"

There was no sign of him. She probably thought I'd had a bad dream. And maybe I did. Except I think I was awake when I had it.

I stumbled back to my bed and fell asleep. Dreams haunted me again. Except it seemed impossible to separate the old nightmares from the new ones. I saw explosions in my head, tinted green. I heard myself groaning, as if I were listening from outside my body. And there were eyes—green bloodshot eyes glaring at me with such hatred. They weren't even human.

I awoke once more in the darkness, afraid the old man would be sitting there again. He wasn't. I staggered to the bathroom, turned on the light, and looked in the mirror.

My face appeared fine, normal.

Then I looked down.

My clothes, my pajamas, were hanging in tatters. Shirt, pajama pants, all ripped at the seams. As if I'd grown too big for them, and then shrunk back down again.

53

How is any of this possible?

Maybe . . . maybe the mad old man *is* my father. Because if my father's insane, then that would explain why I'm going crazy as well.

54

Morning

"Experiments."

The old man talked about some sort of "experiments."

I'm starting to develop a theory. A strange, horrifying theory.

When I checked myself out of the infirmary, I asked Betty to draw a couple of tubes worth of my blood from me. I told her I wanted to run some tests on it. She didn't question my request. After all, she probably felt that if the nanomeds affected my bloodstream, I would probably be one of the few people alive qualified to figure out just what had been done.

She also told me she'd gotten a message from her father, the General. He wanted to see her. I'm not sure whether to be pleased or concerned. Perhaps General Ross can get Talbot off our backs. On the other hand, perhaps he'll make things worse. I didn't say that to Betty, of course. I just told her she'd be fine. And she probably will be.

I don't know if I will be, though.

April 11, 2003

Evening

Impossible. Just impossible.

I conducted experiments on the blood samples all day here in the lab. The gamma radiation is there. The preliminary tests didn't show it, because the radiation is being stored somehow. The cells . . . chemical bonds in the DNA . . . storing too much energy . . . impossible . . . impossible.

We thought it was the nanomeds that had enabled me to survive. But they were only part of it. The frogs weren't able to survive the nanomeds, but I was—I survived the nanomeds. I survived the

57

gamma radiation. Because something is different about my blood. About me.

Betty was right. There's something different about me.

Insane theory. Let's say, just for argument's sake, that the old man wasn't crazy. That he is my father. He talked about experiments. What if *he* did this to me? What if he conducted experiments on me when I was a child. Or what if he did things to himself? An even worse idea, and one that made even more sense. What if he experimented on himself and, because of that, passed on some sort of bizarre condition to me that turned me into this . . . this . . . this what?

What am I?

The phone rang, and the answering machine picked up. It was Betty. She said, "I saw my father. It's like he suspects you of something. Oh, I don't know. I was so impatient, as always. I should have heard him out. I think they're planning something, with the lab. With you. Just call me, okay?"

Planning something. With me. The experiments . . . maybe more experiments, maybe they're all in on it—that crazy old man, Betty's father, Talbot—all working together. They all want something from me. Why don't they leave me alone? *Why don't they just leave me alone?*

Heart's pounding in my head . . . hand trembling . . . getting hard to write, hard to concentrate. My hand . . . what's happening . . . turning . . . green, that can't be right, must be the lighting, must . . .

Betty . . .

April 12, 2003

Morning

I think I'm under arrest.

I woke up this morning, my head swimming. I expected to find myself in the lab. Instead I was lying in my bed, the bed sheets all twisted around me, my clothes gone. My bedroom looked like a disaster area, things all over the place.

The sun was creeping through the windows, and in the distance I thought I heard fire trucks and ambulances. It was like the whole area had gone crazy.

I closed my eyes, trying to recall what had

happened at the lab the night before. I remember . . . pain. So much pain. And then . . . him. The old man. He was there, reaching toward me, but it wasn't me he was reaching toward, it was . . . somebody else.

Like I was someone else.

My own mind, trapped inside someone else's body.

And this other . . . being I was trapped inside was filled with so much anger and rage. I don't know who he was. Or *what*?

I reached for the remote control, squinting against the sunlight, and turned on the local TV news station. There were emergencies, all right. Some sort of destruction at the lab last night, where I'd been. Something had torn through the roof. That same something had ripped apart parked cars, knocked over trees. Authorities were claiming it was a series of freak tornadoes, but other people were saying they'd seen something—something huge. Something green.

I pulled on some sweatpants, tried to head out into the living room, but it was like my legs had turned to jelly. I fell back into bed, barely had enough strength to turn off the TV with the remote, and went back to sleep. The next thing I knew, Betty was there, calling my name. I thought she was a dream at first.

I pulled myself together and showered. It made me feel a little more human. Then we went out into the dining room and sat down at the table, and I told her everything. I had to. How could I not?

Really, I should have told her earlier. But it's all been so crazy. What would I have said to her? "My father showed up, and he's insane, and by the way, I think the gamma radiation combined with something in my blood causes me to turn into a monster when I'm upset"?

Well, actually, that is what I told her. I told her everything I knew, or thought I knew, up to when I had awoken this morning. She didn't go running, screaming out the door, which was nice, because that's certainly what I felt like doing.

Betty told me the local news hadn't even reported half of the destruction that had occurred at the lab. Things had been smashed to pieces inside and out. Our facilities were still working, but barely. When I told her of my half-remembered encounter with my father, she said, "Then you *were* there, at the lab?"

"No, not me. Something," I said. I felt totally lost. "Betty . . . what's happening to me?"

"Maybe *he* could tell you," said Betty, and I knew which "he" she meant. My father.

Before we could finish the conversation, though, there was a loud pounding at my front door. Betty went and opened it, and in marched several army men identified as MPs—military police—by their armbands. In front of them was a tall, barrel-chested man with a white mustache and enough medals on his jacket front to decorate a Christmas tree. The stars on his shoulders identified him as a general, and I didn't need the look of surprised recognition on Betty's face to tell me that this was her father, "Thunderbolt" Ross.

"Mitchell, escort my daughter downstairs. I'll join her shortly," Ross said. Betty didn't want to go, but I assured her I would be okay, which I didn't completely believe, frankly.

He asked me if I was Bruce Krenzler. I said I was.

"I think you left something at your lab last night," he said.

He held up the torn backseat of a pair of pants and pulled out what I immediately realized was my wallet.

That's when I knew I was in trouble. The only question was, how much trouble was I in?

Evening

They've been at me the whole day.

Around and around they've gone, asking the same questions over and over, trying to trick me. Every time they called me "Dr. Krenzler," they did it with such contempt, as if they knew the name itself was a lie.

What if it is? What if I'm a lie? What if everything I know, or thought I knew, is a lie?

Ross acted as if I were playing some sort of game with them. "You guys buying this repressed-memory syndrome routine?" he asked his soldiers at one point, after grilling me yet again about my youth. He wasn't willing to accept that it was all a blank to me—that I remember almost nothing before my teen years, and certainly not from before I was adopted.

"How many times do I have to tell you?" I asked. "I'd like to help you, but I don't know."

Ross leaned in close to me. He was a cigar smoker. I could tell. The stench of cigars on his breath almost knocked me out. "You know who I am, right, Banner?"

Banner. He called me Banner. The same name that the old man used.

My mind whirling with the notion of the impossible becoming real, I muttered a response. He came in even closer and said, "Let's cut to the chase. I'm the guy who had your father tossed away. And I'll do the same to you if I feel so inclined, you understand?"

"My father. You say his name is Banner?" I asked.

That seemed to encourage him, as if I were admitting to something. Except all I was doing was repeating the names he'd given me. And suddenly he said, "Don't play me. You were four years old when you saw it."

"Saw what?" I asked.

He raised his voice, bellowed at me, "You were right there! How could anyone forget a thing like that?"

"*What?*" I shouted back at him, feeling like my head was splitting apart.

"Oh, some more repressed memories?" he said sarcastically.

I felt broken, used up. "Just tell me," I moaned, and sank down into the chair.

He stared down at me. After an entire day of hammering away at me, I think he was finally starting to believe me. "I'm sorry, son. You're an even more screwed-up mess than I thought you'd be." Then he told me that if I ever came within a thousand yards of Betty, he'd put me away for the rest of my natural life.

I'm not sure how this day could get any worse.

April 13, 2003

Yesterday was . . .

I'm not quite sure how to describe it. I don't remember much of it. But I've managed to figure out everything that happened, and will put it down here as best as I humanly can.

Humanly. Is that a word that even applies to me anymore?

First thing's first.

Late last night, Ross and his men apparently decided to give me a break from yelling at me about things I couldn't remember. As I sat slumped on my couch, bone-weary, mentally exhausted, I thought I was hearing things, a ringing phone. But it didn't sound like my phone.

I rummaged around and found a tiny cell phone shoved into the cushions of the couch. For a moment I thought Ross had left it. Out of curiosity, I answered it.

"Bruce," came a familiar voice, and it was like a cold fist around the base of my spine. It was him. It was the man who claims he is my father. The man who—if Ross could be believed (and why would he lie?)—*is* my father.

"What's wrong with me?" I whispered. "What did you do to me? You experimented on yourself, didn't you? And passed on to me—what?"

"A deformity, you could call it," he said. "But an amazing strength too. And now, unleashed, I can finally harvest it."

"You'll do no such thing," I told him, keeping my voice down so Ross's men outside wouldn't hear me. "I will isolate it and treat it myself. Remove it, kill it, before it does any real harm."

"Oh, I bet you and your Betty would love to destroy it. But would you really, even if it meant

69

killing yourself? I don't think so. And as for Betty . . . I'm sending her a little surprise visit, from some four-legged friends of mine."

I felt panic start to seize me, and fought it away. Chortling, my "father" told me how he had obtained some DNA of mine from the lab and used it to experiment on those . . . those monstrous dogs of his. And Betty—poor, sweet Betty—she had tracked him down, gone to his house to talk to him. To try to understand him, probably in hope of understanding, in turn, what he had done to me.

Instead, she'd set herself up. She'd left behind a scarf, and Banner—apparently that was his last name—had used it to give his monstrous mutants her scent.

They were going to go after her, tear her to bits.

"You're crazy! I won't let you!" I shouted, and threw down the cell phone. I bolted for the front door, threw it open.

Glen Talbot was standing right there.

I tried to tell him Betty was in trouble. That my crazy father had sent gamma-mutated dogs after her. He wouldn't listen. Who would? It all sounded so insane, but it was true.

70

But my father wasn't the only crazy one, as it turned out.

To my shock, Talbot knocked me to the floor. I could barely breathe as he shoved his shoe against my face and snarled, "You pathetic freak! Tomorrow, after I convince Ross, you'll be carted off to spend the rest of your life in some tiny solitary hole. And I'll be able to take over your work!"

I tried to fight back, but he was far stronger than me, and a former army man, trained in hand-to-hand combat. He kicked me and I rolled away, and in the back of my mind, it was like there was another voice in there, another person rooting around, growling, *"Get him! Get him!"*

And I felt as if that other voice, that other person, was the source of all my rage.

The world was starting to blur around me, but I wasn't losing consciousness. Something else was happening.

"Talbot, you're making me angry," I managed to say.

"Oh? Am I?" he asked, looking so smug.

I managed a nod and said, "I don't think you'd like me when I'm angry."

He leaned in to punch me in the gut.

71

I caught his hand, and held it tight. He tried to move it. He couldn't.

The look of astonishment on his face filled me with a dark, almost frightening joy, and then the world around me turned green. I felt pain ripping through my body, saw my arms starting to widen, to twist and distort. Every muscle was on fire. I opened my mouth to scream, and a roar louder than a dozen lions was ripped from my throat.

I was gone.

The creature had arrived.

Rumors had begun circulating about it, about *him*. Someone had claimed to see a great, hulking monster leaping around town, leaving destruction wherever it had been. Some news reporter started calling it "the Hulk," and the name stuck.

Talbot had the chance to see, firsthand, why the creature had been dubbed "the Hulk."

He fell back onto the couch, screaming. The men could hear his shouts outside, and started to head into the house, when suddenly the couch—with Talbot still clutching it—came crashing through the wood and glass of the front window. It had been propelled by a single kick from a massive green foot and had sailed through the air to land heavily on the front lawn, scattering soldiers in all directions.

The Hulk smashed right through the front wall of the house, as if there were a door there and he'd simply opened it. He stood there a moment, then raised his huge green arms above his head and roared a challenge.

The military police started firing. The bullets bounced off his skin, irritating him as if they were wasp stings, but not harming him beyond that.

Leaping at his attackers, the Hulk sent them running. They kept looking over their shoulders as they went, probably to make certain the Hulk wasn't following them.

He wasn't. His mind—although *mind* might be too generous a word—was elsewhere.

Some fragment of the man I was, some tiny bit of my consciousness and concern, was now rumbling around at the base of his brain, just as he had been in mine. All that concern was focused on one thing: Betty.

From the farthest corners of my awareness, the image of the cabin in the woods presented itself. I had suspected Betty would be there, since her own home would probably be surrounded by soldiers and

73

MPs, courtesy of her worrying father. But her father might not know about the cabin, and as a result, she would foolishly believe it to be safe.

Except it wasn't safe. Because I knew that my "father" was sending three (or maybe more!) gamma-irradiated hounds after Betty. And since it was uppermost in *my* thoughts, apparently it was a priority for the Hulk as well.

The Hulk drew a breath and then leaped upward. He was gone in a heartbeat.

Unaware of any of this, of course, was Betty.

She was in her cabin alone. Betty told me that she had long grown accustomed to all the routine sounds that creatures in the forest would make at night. So when something else was out there, something different, it alerted her almost instantly.

Most other women—heck, most other people—would have cowered in their home, waiting for daylight and hoping that whatever was out there would just go away.

Not Betty. Nothing daunted her. Or so she liked to believe.

She flipped on the cabin's exterior lights even as she stepped out into the night air, flashlight in hand.

"Hello?" she called, playing the beam across the circle of redwood trees yards away. The light passed over several trees, and then she suddenly moved the beam back when she realized one of the trees looked different.

It was wider, and smoother.

And greener.

Slowly she moved the flashlight up, trying to keep her hand from shaking, and the light shone upon the burning green eyes of the Hulk.

Betty let out a scream, dropped the flashlight, and backed up. As she did so, she slipped and almost fell . . . but then, to her complete shock, the Hulk swept in with one massive arm and broke her fall.

He eased her to her feet and she stared into his eyes, feeling as if there were something in there that she recognized.

Suddenly the Hulk's nostrils flared as he sniffed the air, growling as if scenting some sort of menace nearby. Betty looked around, wide-eyed, trying to see into the darkness but not spotting anything. She was so startled by the entire thing that part of her was wondering if she were dreaming.

And that was when the dogs came crashing out into the open.

Dogs? No. Not dogs. Not really.

Monsters.

Huge, slavering, wild-eyed. They pounded across the open space, coming straight at the Hulk and Betty, crazed and making barking noises that sounded like a hundred motorcycles backfiring.

The Hulk's back was against Betty's car, and he pushed her into it, slamming shut the door behind her so hard that he half-crushed it inward. Then he turned to face the dogs.

They paused a moment, growling, and for half a heartbeat, Betty thought they were going to withdraw.

She was wrong.

They came in fast and furious, and the Hulk leaped straight up, up, and out of sight. The dogs stopped, confused, barking at one another as if they were accusing each other of having done something with their prey.

Then they turned their attention back to Betty. She saw the power in their bodies, and she had no doubt they could rip the doors off with their teeth.

That was when she heard a whistling sound, like

76

a bomb dropping through the air, and then the Hulk descended from overhead. He hadn't run off or retreated. Instead he'd jumped straight up, and now he was smashing straight back down onto one of the dogs. Strangely, the dog dissolved into what appeared to be a huge puddle. Now there were only two dogs left to deal with.

The dogs turned and sprang toward the Hulk. One of them clamped onto the Hulk's ankle, the other onto his neck.

The Hulk twisted, shook them off, and then vaulted up into a tree, out of their reach. They circled the tree for a moment, tried to leap up after him but failed. So again they turned their attention to Betty.

She cowered back in her car as one of them leaped onto the hood and slammed its paws against the windshield. Weblike cracks ribboned across it. One more slam from those powerful forelegs, and the creatures would be thrusting their jaws into the car.

Suddenly a huge shadow fell behind the dog, and before it had time to react, the Hulk was there. He was holding an enormous tree that he had obviously uprooted, and he swung it around. The dog slammed

77

into the windshield. Betty was certain the dog was dead.

In the meantime, the Hulk was wrestling around on the ground with the third and largest dog. They were like two animals spat out from some prehistoric time, rolling about and snarling, neither making noises that sounded remotely human.

Betty started to lean forward to get a better look at what was happening outside and abruptly let out a scream—the dog that was crushed against the windshield turned out to be very much alive. Its eyes widened as it thrust its head forward, sending glass shards onto Betty's lap. She screamed—the last noise she thought she would ever make.

But that one final lunge had been the last act the dog was capable of. The creature began to melt, dissolving before her eyes. Betty made a noise of utter disgust, and turned to see the final moments of the Hulk's struggle with the last dog. She couldn't believe it. She saw the animal literally sink its teeth into the back of the Hulk's neck . . . and the Hulk's neck muscles rippled, grew, and forced the beast's teeth right back out. The Hulk's massive hands clamped around the dog. The last of the attacking animals dissolved.

Then the Hulk staggered forward, looking exhausted. His breathing slowed, fatigue creeped in, and also perhaps a sense of relief that he had done what he'd set out to do.

Betty was safe . . . because of him.

And as if the now falling rain were washing him away, the Hulk himself began to dissolve. For an instant, Betty thought the Hulk was going to go the way of the creatures he'd just destroyed, of which nothing was left.

She received quite a shock when she saw me there in the Hulk's place.

As for me . . . the events of the previous hours were a blur.

I remembered Talbot hitting me, and I remembered the beginnings of the transformation. I had a brief fragment of memory of Talbot hurtling through the window of my home, clutching on to the couch for dear life. I remembered the ground fading beneath me as the Hulk sailed high through the air. And I recalled flashes of the battle with the dogs.

79

Everything else was buried under a haze of instinct and rage. Even when I remembered things, it was as if I were recalling events of someone else's life. As if I'd watched it through a telescope.

I didn't know whether to laugh or cry, and did a combination of both.

I approached Betty. I made a fist, punched the air, and came a little too close to Betty's face. I didn't notice. Instead I started babbling. I must have sounded like a crazy man.

"Am I awake? Was it me? I killed them, right? I killed them!"

Then, totally forgetting about Betty's nightmares in which she'd dreamed I was trying to hurt her, I put my hand over her mouth, and said, "Like that! I snapped their necks!"

She shouted my name and pushed me away. Immediately I felt terrible, remembering those nightmares she'd had, realizing what I'd done.

Thank heavens, I think she understood. Very softly, she said, "You can't control it, can you?" I shook my head. "Do you remember how it comes?" she asked.

Again I shook my head, and stared at my fist as

if it were somebody else's. She took it gently in her hands.

I was so tired. She brought me into the cabin, cleaned me up. More than anything, I just wanted to go to sleep, but I knew if I didn't write down everything that had happened immediately, I might forget it all. So she brought me paper and a pen, and I made this entry, even though my eyes were trying to close. Even though I felt as if I had no energy left to write. As I wrote, I worked with Betty to fill in the gaps of what had happened, so I could make this entry as complete as possible.

If I don't remember as many of the details as I can, who else will?

I don't know what's happening to me. It's the anger, the rage. I don't know. I'm just . . . tired. Afraid, and so tired. . . .

April 15?, 2003

The date is a guess. I'm not sure of anything. I've lost track of days.

I should have filed my income taxes, if today is in fact the 15th. I didn't. Yet I'm not at all concerned about getting in trouble, because I don't think I can get into any more trouble than I'm in right now.

It started the morning after the dogs attacked Betty.

The sun was up and the day was so peaceful and quiet that it was hard to believe there had been such violence mere hours before. Betty and I were sipping coffee in the cabin's small kitchen, discussing my situation.

Betty was speculating that my anger triggered a change in my DNA, causing tremendous amounts of energy to be released. She also speculated, frighteningly enough, that it was possible for the transformation to continue. That it could result in a chain reaction that would cause me—cause the Hulk—to just keep growing and growing. It was a terrifying notion.

"You know what scares me the most?" I admitted to her, "When it happens . . . when it comes over me, when I totally lose control . . . I like it."

A look passed over her face. She seemed frightened. Why shouldn't she have been? I was.

Then there was some sort of noise outside. Something stepping on a branch, breaking it, and something else causing leaves to rustle.

I went to a window to look outside.

There was a popping sound and I looked down. Something had flown through the air and landed squarely in my stomach. It was still quivering there, and I recognized it instantly.

It was a knockout dart. A tranquilizer.

83

Even as I realized it, all the strength vanished from my legs. Then Betty was by my side, and she didn't seem the least bit surprised as she eased me to the floor.

My mind still hadn't processed what was happening, and then Betty was speaking into my ear so quickly, the words tumbling over one another.

"It's going to be all right. It's just going to make you sleep. You'll forgive me, Bruce. I know you will. I didn't know what else to do to help you, okay? We're going someplace safe, where nothing can come after you. You understand. I didn't know what to do. I couldn't just let you go."

And just as I slipped into unconsciousness, I saw a gas-masked tactical team in army uniforms burst through the door.

That's when I realized what was happening.

Betty had called her father.

She'd been so afraid of me that she'd gone to a man she couldn't stand for help and protection.

When I awoke, I found myself in a small room. A cell, really. It's where I am right now. Men are marching around outside wearing uniforms, and glancing in at me suspiciously, as if they think I'm suddenly going to turn huge and green and tear them apart.

I don't know where I am. I don't know *what* I am. And yet everyone's afraid of me, and they all seem to want to know what I know, which isn't much.

What have I turned into?

April 16?, 2003

I'm underground at Desert Base, as it turns out. I'm not even aware of the passage of day and night anymore. I sleep when I get tired. The rest of the time I stay awake, make entries into my journal, and just think about things.

I've had several visitors. One of them was "Thunderbolt" Ross. He started asking me about my father again, very suspiciously. It seemed as if he were trying to determine whether I'd had some fore-knowledge of David (that being his first name) Banner's activities.

Ross himself wasn't completely forthcoming, but reading between the lines, I was able to figure out that Banner had definitely been up to something. Apparently there had been some sort of further activity back at the lab, more use of the gamma equipment. Things had been smashed up, and a guard was killed. They didn't know for sure that my so-called father had been involved, but they had their suspicions.

That was, however, all they had. I couldn't provide them with any more information. How would it have been possible? I was cooped up in a cell. It seemed to me as if they were ready to blame me for just about anything.

Still, the notion that my father might be out there, getting into the gamma equipment, doing who knows what with it, bothered me a great deal. On the other hand, with any luck he'd kill himself with radiation poisoning, and I'd never have to worry about that strange, demented man again.

Odd. Ross knew that Banner had sicced those dogs on Betty. He also knew that I—at least, I as the Hulk—had saved her life.

He never thanked me. How's that for gratitude?

Hours later (I couldn't say how many), Betty came by. She didn't seem to want to look me in the eye. I think she was embarrassed about what had happened. She was the first one to tell me that we were in an underground research facility at Desert Base—the same place where she had grown up and where, supposedly, I had grown up as well.

She said she told her father that the key to my controlling these changes—presuming it's possible to control them at all—was to take the emotional conditions that triggered the change and connect them to the memories they're linked to. She believes I possess anger so overwhelming that it literally causes me to transform, and if I understand what generates the anger, I can defuse it before it changes me into a monster. Then she told me she was working on arranging something that might cause those memories to return.

I wish I knew whether that was a good thing or a bad thing.

April 17, 2003

When I first emerged from the hidden exit to the underground Desert Base, I blinked furiously against the brightness of the sun. The heat of the desert slammed into me like a fist. I had to draw in a few deep gulps of air just to be able to catch my breath.

Betty smiled, looking as if she was just happy to be there. I wasn't sure if she felt that way because she was eager to help me, or because she finally felt as if she had returned home.

As homecomings go, it didn't have much of a datelike atmosphere . . . probably because of the two dozen soldiers following not ten paces behind us. They were armed with various high-tech containment weapons and were watching for the slightest hint of my undergoing a transformation.

Betty and I walked through what had once been, according to her, a section of town with many stores and shops. All that remained of them was an assortment of burned-out buildings. I was still vague on exactly what had happened, and Betty didn't seem anxious to tell me. Perhaps she thought it would be too much to hit me with all at once. But I was getting the sick and distressing feeling that whatever had obliterated an entire base, whatever had turned this area into little more than a ghost town, it had something to do with my father.

My father.

I found myself thinking of him in that way more and more. Was I really accepting the notion that a homicidal madman had truly sired me?

Betty told me that federal agents had gone to the house where he'd been staying, or hiding, or whatever you'd call the existence he was leading. He wasn't there. Instead they found research equipment that they didn't understand . . . along with a large, snarling green rat that attacked them, which they did understand. They shot the rodent, although they couldn't comprehend why the thing was so grotesque.

I, however, could. So could Betty.

"It used to be so full of life here," said Betty as we continued to walk down the street. The soldiers dutifully followed us. She smiled at me playfully and cast a glance in their direction. "What do you think those boys would do if I leaned over and gave you a kiss?"

"I'm not sure either of us would survive," I said.

We stopped walking and stood there, face-to-face, and stared at each other uncomfortably. I shook my head. "I must have seen you or known you. If only I could remember."

"You will," she said gently, putting a hand on my arm. "It'll be painful, but you will."

I thought of the huge green monster that dwelled within me. "I bet *it* remembers," I growled. "It must have been a child here too, inside of me. I feel him now, watching me, hating me."

She looked bewildered. "Hating you? Why?"

"Because," I said grimly, "he knows, one way or another, that we're going to destroy him."

"We're going to *understand* him," she said, correcting me.

I shrugged. "It's the same thing, isn't it?"

She had no response to that. She knew I was right.

We found an abandoned swing set and Betty sat on one of the swings, idly pushing herself back and forth. I didn't pay attention, however, because I was looking elsewhere, at a particular house nearby. The moment I saw it, it seemed . . . familiar. I started toward it. I heard the swing cease its squeaking. Betty had gotten off it and was following me.

I entered the old house, squinting in the darkness. The place was musty, cobwebs everywhere, bugs scuttling into the shadows the moment I walked in.

I felt a sudden rush of frustration. It was as if another entire life was hidden just behind a curtain, and either I wasn't able to pull it aside . . . or wasn't sure if I should. Turning to Betty, I said, "Why did you bring me here? What's the point of it? You saw what I am. You know as well as I do it's no use."

"That's not true," she said firmly.

"It is true," I replied. "I'm supposed to have some sort of emotional breakthrough now? Reconnect to my inner child, exorcise my inner demons, find my true self, and everything will be just fine and dandy?" I shook my head. "Don't kid yourself."

She walked across the room to face me. "And don't kid *yourself*! We don't have any options, remember? At least here—" she gestured around the house, "we have a chance. . . . "

"A chance to what?" I demanded. "Don't you understand? Whatever it is you want me to remember, there's a good reason I can't. It might just kill me."

"Or save you."

"And what if I don't want to be saved?" I asked, feeling sorry for myself.

"You don't have to try. You can choose, Bruce. But me, I don't have a choice, okay?"

"Why?" I asked sadly.

She sighed heavily, as if admitting a frustrating truth. "Because I love you."

It was so strange to me, that she would say that. "How is that possible?" I asked. "You—neither of us—we don't even know who I am."

I turned away from her and kicked through the rubble a bit. She went to a broken window and stared out at the desert.

I told her we'd better go back, and she agreed.

So back I went, exchanging the prison of my mind for the prison of a cell in the underground base.

I wonder how long they think they can keep me cooped up like this. I'm an American citizen. I have rights.

Except . . . maybe I don't. After all, monsters don't have rights. Mad dogs don't have rights. Earthquakes and hurricanes don't have rights.

I'm starting to think of myself as less human and more as a pure force of destruction.

Maybe it would be better if I never got out of here.

April 18, 2003

Hurts. Hurts . . . so much.

Talbot's back, and he's not happy.

He came into my cell this morning, still looking bruised and banged up. I knew something had changed when a number of small openings popped out all around me in the wall. Gun barrels. And a dozen red laser dots appeared all over me, making me look as if I had a sudden outbreak of measles. I was targeted from all directions. They were ready if I made the slightest aggressive move.

Based on that, I wasn't entirely surprised when

Talbot walked in. After all, they knew I wouldn't do anything to hurt Betty, and her father was treating me with caution; he wasn't being especially abusive. So if someone was going to be confronting me with reason to think I might hurt him, well . . . the number of people on that list was fairly short, and Talbot was at the top of it.

I knew instantly that the situation had changed. Talbot must have pulled strings. He was running the show now, rather than Betty or her father. Talbot was walking with the swagger of someone who believes he has all the power in a particular situation.

"Hiya, Bruce," he said, with a false heartiness. "How are you feeling? Is the grub here okay for you?"

I ignored what he probably thought was clever conversation. Instead I told him he was looking a little worse for wear. It was true. He had several visible bruises, a neckbrace, and he was walking with what appeared to be a cane. But he shrugged it off, acting as if nothing were wrong.

"What are you doing here?" I asked, already sensing what the answer would be.

He grinned and told me, and it was everything I

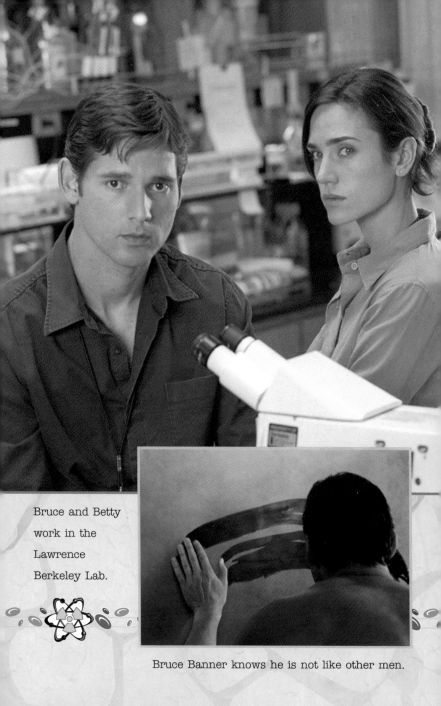

Bruce and Betty work in the Lawrence Berkeley Lab.

Bruce Banner knows he is not like other men.

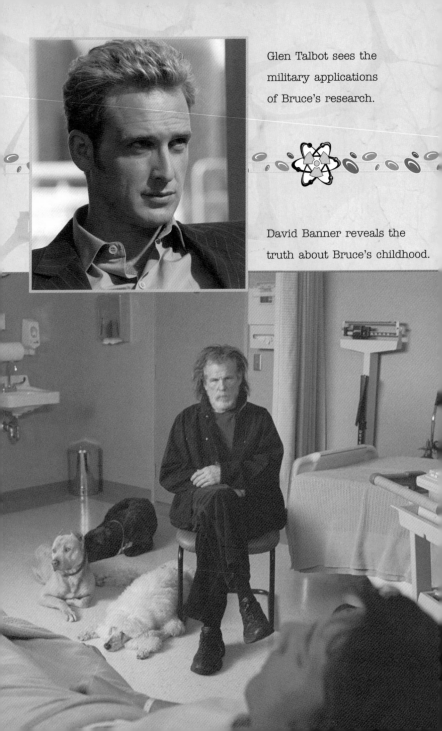

Glen Talbot sees the
military applications
of Bruce's research.

David Banner reveals the
truth about Bruce's childhood.

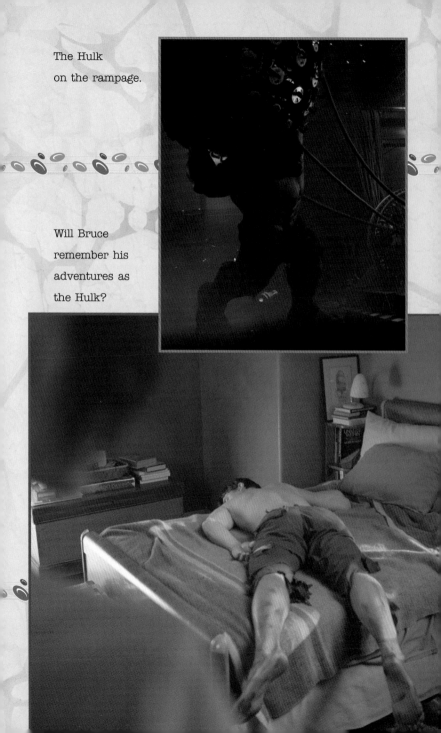

The Hulk
on the rampage.

Will Bruce
remember his
adventures as
the Hulk?

The army keeps Bruce under maximum security.

Can General "Thunderbolt"
Ross contain the Hulk?

The Hulk escapes!

The Hulk charges through the compound.

A tank is no match for the Hulk.

"Thunderbolt" Ross

chases down the Hulk.

The Hulk searches
San Francisco.

Betty brings out
the man inside
the beast.

The Hulk: You won't like him when he's angry.

could do not to show the horror I felt from his answer.

He wanted skin-cell samples from me. Gamma-irradiated cell samples. I could only guess why. To plant in soldiers, perhaps, as he was talking about days ago, except they wouldn't just be fast-healing soldiers. He'd be turning men into monsters.

Maybe he even wanted to find a way to clone the Hulk.

But he had no idea of the forces he was playing with. He only saw the potential for profit for his laboratory. He was blind to the possibility of horrifying destruction.

However, he needed me to transform into the Hulk in order to get what he wanted. My own skin cells weren't enough. He needed the monster's.

I wasn't about to give it to him, and told him so.

"I'm not sure you have much of a choice," he said, and suddenly he jammed his cane forward. It wasn't a cane, or at least not just a cane. It was some sort of electric prod. The moment it touched my skin, I was thrown backward by the force of the jolt. I slammed against the far wall and crumpled to the floor.

"C'mon, Bruce," said Talbot, strolling toward me.

97

"Aren't you feeling a little angry? After all, you have only me to play with, now that Betty's dumped you and gone back to Berkeley."

I glared up at him. "You're lying."

He stopped a foot or so away. "You know, for me this is a win-win situation. You turn green, all these guys kill you, and I perform the autopsy. You don't, I mop the floor with you, and—" he leaned forward and whispered in my ear, "maybe by accident I go too far and break your neck."

He smiled, waiting for me to take that in. "Bad science, maybe," he continued, "but personally gratifying. Come to think of it, you are looking a little green around the gills."

Using the wall for support, I hauled myself to my feet. He waved the cane at me, and I could see the shock probes at the tip. "C'mon . . . just a love tap. Let's see what you've got."

I knew what I had inside me, but I had no intention of putting it on display. "Never," I managed to say. Then I stumbled toward him, still unable to control my muscles. I expected him to hit me with the shock cane again.

I was wrong. He tossed the cane aside and hit me with his fists.

I went down and figured the only thing I had left to do was pretend I was unconscious. So that's what I did, just lying there, saying nothing.

He continued to shout at me even though I made no sound. And then General Ross came in, and I never, ever thought I'd actually be happy to see "Thunderbolt" Ross. Not that he knew I saw him; I was keeping my eyes mostly closed.

"Talbot, that's enough!" shouted Ross.

"All in the name of science, sir," Talbot replied, and swaggered out of the room.

And then I heard him say something about my not being able to control the change if I was unconscious . . . and something else about an immersion tank.

I know what that is, of course. A huge tank, like an oversized bathtub, filled with fluid and then sealed up once the subject is placed inside. You float there like a baby in a mother's womb, except they can hook you up to all sorts of electronics and such and monitor your every breath, your every thought.

99

They can even try to manipulate your consciousness electronically, place ideas in your head. . . .

Make you snap.

It's all so clear.

They're going to try to force me to bring the Hulk
into existence by controlling my mind.

My father isn't the only insane one. They're *all*
crazy.

April ?, 2003

They thought they could control him . . . it . . . us. The fools. The blind fools.

They came for me and hauled me out of my chamber while I was still barely conscious. I suppose they wanted to make sure they didn't get a lot of fight out of me. They needn't have worried. I was aware of my surroundings, but I hadn't gathered the energy to put up any sort of fight. Not that I would have been able to provide much of one, even if I wanted to try.

They strapped me to a table and wheeled me

through the compound as briskly as they could. I tried to raise my head and look around, but it all went by so fast that I barely caught a glimpse of it. There were gleaming metal walls all around, and rooms sectioned off by huge thick doors of clear glass. There was an area set into the wall high above, with scientists in white lab coats staring down through observation windows. Central command, no doubt.

All over the compound, soldiers stopped in their tracks and gaped at me as I was wheeled past. I didn't see Ross anywhere, and I certainly didn't see Betty. I can only imagine what the soldiers were thinking. The Hulk, terror of the military, was this . . . nothing. This scrawny, unimpressive nothing.

Talbot stood there, smiling, as they rolled me up to what I immediately recognized as an immersion tank. I didn't bother to struggle or try to talk him out of it. There was no point. He was too far gone, obsessed with the idea of tapping into the power of the Hulk.

They drugged me to make sure I didn't come to full consciousness and possibly cause problems. Then they attached an array of electrodes to my body and eased me into an immersion tank. The fluid was warm as I sank into it. It really did feel as if I were returning to the womb.

Then the tank was closed.

Absolute darkness surrounded me.

I could see nothing. I floated there, face up. The only things I heard were the gentle splashing of fluid around me, my slow breathing, and—I thought—the sound of my heart beating.

It had been so long since I'd fallen into anything like a deep sleep; I literally could not remember the last time it had happened. But it happened this time. I felt as if I was falling deeper and deeper into my own mind.

Images began to spiral around. Pieces of my life, long buried, started to coalesce for the first time in years. Things that I'd had only the briefest glimpses of finally hung together.

I saw him.

First and foremost, looming across my memories like a dark giant, was David Banner.

If there had been any doubt or, for that matter, any hope that the crazed, terrifying old man who claimed to be my father was lying, this new clarity of vision set it aside. The man whom I'd had brief glimpses of in passing dreams was now there, in front of me in my mind, big as life.

He was thirty years younger than he was when I'd seen him in person in the infirmary, but it was him. Definitely him.

Any number of times in the past, I had seen myself as a child, sitting in the living room of a non-descript house, playing with those two shapeless dolls. And there was a man screaming, face purpling with rage, arguing with a woman . . . a woman who I knew must have been my mother.

The man was David Banner, the woman's face remained unknown to me, and I was there. I, Bruce Banner, saw it, saw my father approach my mother. . . .

No. No . . . he was approaching me, and my mother was in the way.

He was shouting, pointing at me.

"Monster," he was saying.

Waving a knife.

Suddenly I knew. Suddenly it was all clear to me. Things that Ross had said, that David Banner had said, clicked together in my mind like the cogs of wheels meshing and setting a machine—my memory—into order.

My father had worked for the army. Worked there, at Desert Base, with "Thunderbolt" Ross overseeing him.

He had wanted to conduct experiments. Terrible genetic experiments. Ross had forbidden it.

So David Banner had conducted them anyway, on the only test subject he could find—himself.

And then I had come along.

And whatever it was that my father had done, whatever genetic or cellular damage he had inflicted upon himself, had been passed on to me.

Once opened, like a dam no longer holding back water, my memories flooded out. Me as an infant, howling, my arm swelling up, and as a little boy, getting angry at a bully, my skin rippling. The pain had been horrifying, and people who had seen it had been terrified and had run from me. Which meant, even from a young age, I knew—I knew that if I lost my temper, bad things would happen. *Very bad things*.

And there was the worst. My father, coming at me . . . with a knife.

He was appalled by what I had become, by the

creature that he had put on this earth through his experiments. He felt I had to die before I grew up, before I became something much, much worse.

And he was screaming other things at my mother, who was trying to keep him from me.

Telling her that Ross had learned about his experiments.

Telling her that he'd been fired. That the army wanted him gone. That they would pay for getting rid of him. He'd rigged a cyclotron at the Base to explode. He called it his "going away" present.

And he said it was all my fault. That I had to pay, too. Pay like the army was going to pay.

He wasn't making any sense at all.

It seemed so unreal. But the knife was real. And his intention to murder me—that was real, too.

He came at me, swinging his knife, and my mother got in between us, and then she screamed.

She staggered away from him, and there was a look of shock on my father's face. My mother was clutching her side. Blood was welling up between her fingers.

Her blood.

I saw my mother stagger out, away, into the desert.

I ran after her. I was blinded by tears.

And then, suddenly, there were soldiers. Soldiers everywhere.

And General Ross.

And a little girl. Betty. Betty was with him. She saw me, and I her. We locked eyes. We'd met as children, and later as adults, and I hadn't remembered it.

I was howling for my mother, sobbing, and my father was being hauled away.

All the pain, all the anguish came flooding back.

My mind overloaded.

I thrashed about in the tank, and suddenly there was pain everywhere. The rage came for me, the anger, like a thing alive. Like another person throwing his arms around me, embracing me, and I welcomed it. I let it come and was glad that it had finally arrived.

I screamed in the immersion tank, but nobody could hear me. My arms, legs, back . . . it felt as if they were aflame. Like someone jabbing millions of white-hot needles into me. That just made me angrier, the fury fueling itself like a raging fire.

And then I was gone. Only the briefest flashes of what happened next remained with me, viewed through infuriated eyes that saw the world in a haze of vivid green.

The people watching the immersion tank saw the tank crack open, liquid cascading everywhere. There were shouts, and alarms sounded throughout the facility.

Then the tank was ripped apart and the Hulk was standing there, dripping wet and snarling. The tank itself was inside a larger cell, and the Hulk began pounding on the cell walls. His muscles rippled like snakes beneath his skin, and the walls shook violently under the pounding.

Gas started to flood into the chamber. Knockout gas, with the intention of putting the Hulk soundly to sleep so that the watching Talbot could collect his skin samples.

Realizing on some primal level that the gas would take him down, the Hulk doubled his efforts. He started to sag, the gas nearly getting to him. He put all his remaining strength into one desperate strike of his massive fist. It worked. His fist crashed through the wall, tearing a gaping hole. Fresh air rushed in, and the Hulk climbed out.

Armed Atheon security personnel charged down the hallway where they knew the Hulk was rampaging. They came face-to-face with him as they rounded a corner, and one of the technicians stepped forward with a large-barreled gun attached to two tanks on his back.

He fired.

The Hulk had no idea what to expect. He wasn't capable of thinking that coherently. All he knew was that suddenly a stream of gelatinous liquid was blasting out of the end of the gun, enveloping him. Within seconds it started to harden around him, encasing him like a fly in fast-drying glue.

General Ross was seeing it all happen on the screens in front of him. He was in a different section of the underground complex from Talbot, and he was furious. His intention was to send in his own soldiers to take care of a situation that had gotten completely out of hand. Over a radio communications system, he told Talbot angrily, "I want a full-court evacuation now! I'm shutting you down!"

Talbot wasn't about to allow Ross to send in his

own people, nor was he going to let the general shut down anything. Before any of Ross's troops could get there, Talbot, from his control room, sent huge metal doors slamming down, cutting off the entire Atheon section from the rest of the Base. Talbot must have figured that he had the Hulk trapped, and would also be able to keep the soldiers out.

What he hadn't considered was that he had trapped himself and his own people in there, with the Hulk.

Talbot grabbed a laser drill and, accompanied by several of his men, went down to the corridor where the Hulk was being held, immobilized by the quickly hardening foam. The Hulk was still struggling, but it seemed as if he were held fast.

"Now let's take this nice and easy," said Talbot as he brought the laser drill up, determined to get cell samples.

The Hulk let out a scream as the laser penetrated his skin. His anger swelled, and Talbot didn't realize that the angrier Hulk got, the stronger he got.

"Pull back!" Talbot told his people as the Hulk started breaking off huge chunks of hardened foam, shaking them loose. Within seconds the Hulk was free, stomping down the hallway after them.

Talbot and his Atheon soldiers fled down a corridor. It was sealed off at the far end by one of the large metal doors, but then the door slid open. Ross's soldiers were on the other side, about to charge in and take over the operation. They probably figured they could succeed where Atheon's security force had failed.

Talbot must not have wanted to let that happen. He grabbed a huge gun out of the hands of one of his own people, turned, and faced the Hulk. The monster was approaching them, the floor trembling under his feet.

The Hulk and Talbot faced each other. It was like a scene from the distant past, a primitive hunter squaring off against a towering, furious mammoth, hoping his weaponry would offset the difference in pure power.

The Hulk roared and started to grow. Talbot stepped back, blinking, as the Hulk grew from twelve feet to fifteen feet. He was practically taking up all of the corridor. There was no way Talbot could possibly miss; a blind man could have hit the Hulk at that point.

"So long, big boy," said Talbot.

He started shooting, spraying the Hulk with a hail of powerful automatic fire.

The Hulk doubled over in pain as the bullets hit him.

They bounced off him.

Talbot realized his mistake, but it was too late. The ricocheting bullets hit Talbot. He was dead.

The soldiers stood frozen at the far end of the hallway, having seen what had just happened.

They didn't hesitate.

They ran.

They ran as fast as they humanly could, and the Hulk stormed after them. The metal door slammed down the second they were through, closing off the approaching Hulk.

The soldiers thought they were safe . . . or at least they did for as long as it took the metal door to start buckling beneath the Hulk's savage onslaught.

Realizing he and the soldiers didn't have much time, Ross had his people roll in a gigantic array of powerful strobe lights. The instant the enraged Hulk smashed through, he was greeted with a blast of illumination as powerful as a hundred thousand flashbulbs set off all at once.

He reeled back, flailing his arms, trying not to lose his balance, trying to find something that he could smash or hit. The world must have been a sea of white to him, and the soldiers took that opportunity to lunge, shooting weighted bolo nets designed to bring him down.

It didn't work.

The instant his huge, questing fingers came in contact with the nets, he yanked them clear and flung them back at the soldiers. He swayed forward, and his eyes began to focus on the troops as they retreated, indicating that his vision was recovering far more quickly than they anticipated. Before they could reignite the strobes, the Hulk pounded the ceiling, sending huge support beams crumbling and falling across the length of the hall. One of them crashed downward and destroyed the strobe array. The Hulk lurched, off balance, but still coming.

The Hulk made it to the tunnel that led to the surface. The soldiers massed flamethrowers and let loose a barrage of fire at him. It didn't even begin to slow him down. He only grunted at an assault that would have been hot enough to melt a dozen automobiles.

Seconds later, the Hulk smashed his way to the surface. There was a movie screen there from an old, deserted drive-in theater; it collapsed as the ground shook beneath it. When the Hulk stood there, it was as if some old movie monster had come to life and had stepped right off the silver screen, destroying it as he went.

He stood there in the desert, blinking against the sun. He paused, and then leaped away.

He came down in the old neighborhood that had once housed a child named Bruce Banner. He saw my old house, squinted at the window. I know he did, because it's one of the few moments of his rampage I remember clearly, the small part of me within his mind surfacing to see the dusty interior of my old house.

Just for a moment, it was as if our minds . . . connected somehow. I saw my past through his eyes, and he saw his present through mine. I was appalled by the sheer ferocity of his personality, if one can call pure rage a "personality." And yet, at the same time, I was attracted to it. Even relieved a bit. Finally, finally all the emotion, everything I'd bottled up for so long was out, like a volcano spewing forth lava.

It felt good. Heaven help me, it felt good.

And suddenly I disappeared, spiraled away once more, as a barrage of bombs landed, turning the entire old neighborhood into a wall of flame.

The Hulk was blasted back by the force of the bombs. He landed hard in the desert dunes, sending up a plume of sand. He staggered to his feet, growling with a sound like an approaching locomotive, and saw army assault vehicles hurtling across the desert surface.

One of the vehicles had a machine gunner mounted on the back. Unfortunately, it also had a tow chain in the front. The Hulk bolted forward, snagged the chain in one massive hand, drew it taut, and hauled the vehicle into the air. He whipped it around in a circle, the gunner firing down at him in ever-widening arcs and having no effect.

The soldiers dropped out of the vehicle an instant before the Hulk released it, sending it flying.

It landed on one of several Abrams tanks that were fast approaching, bringing the attacking vehicle to a halt. Even as that happened, the Hulk sprang, landed on the tank, and twisted off the gun turrets. He pried it open as if it were a can of soda and then upended it. The soldiers tumbled out, took one look at the monster raging over them, and ran.

More ground troops were approaching, but when they saw what the Hulk was doing with one of their most powerful vehicles—tossing it from hand to hand like a toy—they pulled back.

General Ross was already on the phone with the President of the United States and the National Security Advisor. "I need everything we have at my disposal to stop his movement," Ross told them.

"General, are you expecting civilian casualties?" asked the National Security Advisor.

"Not if I can help it."

"Consider it done," said the President.

Moments later, Ross was in pursuit of the Hulk. In a Black Hawk helicopter, he hurtled toward the scene of the conflict. He was soon above the battle site, except there was no battle. There was just the Hulk, moving across the desert at high speed, running and jumping and going faster and faster with every moment. Despite the speed of the Black Hawk, it took the Hulk less than a minute to leave Ross behind, much to the general's astonishment.

The Hulk moved far across the southwest landscape. Sensing that there was no one behind him, a momentary wave of calm swept through him.

He came to a halt atop a landscape of steep cliffs and rock formations. Looking across that vast and endless vista, the sea of turmoil that was his thoughts began to subside. Once again I rose to consciousness within him, sensed his thoughts however distantly. On the one hand, he seemed to revel in the anger that caused him to exist. On the other, it was almost as if he were seeking out a place of peace so that he could be left alone . . . without truly comprehending that if he found it, he would go away.

Or perhaps he did comprehend it. Perhaps, on some level, he hated the circumstances that led to his very existence.

Unfortunately, the army didn't give him a chance to find out.

Four Comanche choppers rose from the valley below, hovering directly in front of him.

The Hulk reached out and grabbed one of the

117

moving propellers from the closest chopper. It swung into him, and he took ahold of and wrestled its tail. Together the chopper and the Hulk rolled down the side of the cliff, the screeching of the twisting metal nearly drowned out by the infuriated roars of the Hulk.

The other choppers regrouped as the Hulk picked himself up and clambered up the embankment. He vaulted from one outcropping of rock to the next as the choppers came in after him.

Seconds later he was clambering up a canyon wall as the Comanches blasted away.

He reached the top of a ledge on a large outcropping just as one of the Comanches fired a missile. It struck just to the Hulk's left, blowing off the entire outcropping and sending the Hulk and the ledge tumbling down.

Down, but unhurt.

The Hulk wasn't slowing, but the Comanches were. The helicopters were running low on fuel and were forced to break off the attack. The Hulk, of course, had fuel to spare. Without a backward glance, he vaulted into the sky, hurtling right over

Ross's Black Hawk, toward the general direction of Ross's worst nightmare scenario: heavily populated San Francisco.

As Ross alerted the mayor of San Francisco that a large, green visitor was on his way, the army caught up with the Hulk as he hurtled across the Sierra Nevadas. Three F-22 Raptor jets fell into pursuit behind him.

They chased him all the way to the Marin Headlands, overlooking the Golden Gate Bridge and San Francisco itself, sprawled at the bridge's far end. The jets buzzed the Hulk, as if trying to warn him back.

He didn't heed the warning.

Instead, with a thrust of his powerful leg muscles, he leaped toward the bridge. Seconds later, he landed atop one of the arches and turned to face his pursuers.

One of the planes had cut a bit too close to the bridge in order to avoid a helicopter. Without hesitation, the Hulk jumped onto the plane, landing squarely on top of it and wrapping his huge arms around the fuselage. The plane was forced down,

119

swooping below the bridge instead of hitting it. The Hulk's back scraped the bottom of the bridge, creasing it as he passed under.

Seizing the opportunity, the pilot barreled the plane heavenward. The Hulk, powered by sheer stubbornness rather than common sense, held on instead of letting go. Up through the clouds, far higher than anything that could be approached by one of the Hulk's leaps. Ice began to encrust the Hulk's skin as the air thinned.

Even the Hulk needed to be able to breathe. His eyes fluttered shut. His arms went limp.

He slid off the plane.

He tumbled through the air, fading into unconsciousness. As he did, our split minds began to drift toward each other.

My repressed thoughts mixed together with his, creating dreamlike visions in my mind's eye.

I saw myself looking in the mirror, shaving, the razor scraping slowly across my face. The Hulk's eyes glared back at me from the mirror. Suddenly the mirror glass flew apart. The Hulk's hand reached out, grabbed me by the neck, and smashed my face back into the mirror.

Incredibly, I started to pry his fingers apart, but then he drove a huge fist toward me, and there was no way to stop it.

I blacked out once more, and then the Hulk crashed into the San Francisco Bay.

The dark waters closed over him, and he sank to the bottom like a block of cement. General Ross, in his Black Hawk, swooped down, circling, but there was no movement from beneath the water.

Suddenly the surface broke and there was the Hulk, gasping for air. Like a whale, he inhaled and then dropped underneath the water once more as the helicopter dove downward, machine-gun fire exploding into the water.

It made no difference. The Hulk was already down deep, hitting the floor of the bay. There he spotted underwater drains that flowed into the city, and he angled himself into them with powerful thrusts of his arms.

Ross was more than frustrated over having lost his target. He was afraid of the options left to him. He was faced with the very real possibility of having to bomb downtown San Francisco if the Hulk re-emerged there. Ross might have to kill thousands of

121

civilians to prevent the Hulk from killing thousands more. It was not a pleasant choice for the General.

In the meantime, the Hulk was rampaging beneath the streets of San Francisco.

At first people must have thought an earthquake was coming to their famous city, home to great, steep, hilly streets and to renowned cable cars gliding along their tracks. Cracks started to appear in the streets, widening with each passing second. Water mains began to break and pedestrians jumped out of the way. At each fire hydrant, caps flew off and water started spouting.

Inside the water drains, the Hulk pushed up with his elbows, punching his way through. Finally, he poked his head up through a manhole cover into the light of day.

He emerged onto the streets at a steep intersection. Dripping wet and not looking especially happy from wading through the San Francisco sewer system, the Hulk glared at the stunned onlookers.

Then he let out a roar that some people later swore caused the very earth to tremble.

Naturally they ran.

This made it difficult for the police and soldiers,

122

who were heading against the flow of the stampeding crowd. They were trying to move toward the Hulk, while everyone else in the area was determined to put as much distance between the Hulk and themselves as possible.

The Hulk raised his arms and bellowed defiance as armed men swept in from all directions. A fleet of helicopters arced through the air. On the ground, the National Guard and hundreds of soldiers and police flooded into the area. SWAT teams scaled the buildings overhead and were hanging out of windows, taking positions on rooftops, targeting the Hulk.

No one was getting any nearer than two hundred feet of the Hulk. They were heavily armed, but they weren't stupid.

None of them had the slightest idea what would happen if all that artillery opened fire. Perhaps it would have been enough concentrated firepower to penetrate the formidable skin of the Hulk. On the other hand, it might have just infuriated him even more. He might have grown to *T. rex*–sized proportions, crushed people beneath his feet, torn down entire buildings with one gargantuan hand. And the ricocheting bullets might well have killed everyone

123

who was shooting at him. It had the potential to be the largest disaster of any single gun battle in modern history.

And then . . . slowly . . . the crowd parted.

And Betty approached.

At her insistence, her father had picked her up in his helicopter and brought her to the heart of the conflict. Now, unarmed but unafraid, Betty walked carefully toward the Hulk, making no sudden moves.

The Hulk saw her.

Never had so many people held their breath simultaneously.

Then the green-skinned monster let out a cry of pain and shame.

Betty continued to move toward him. She reached out, and the Hulk, who might well have withstood a barrage of gunfire from hundreds of armed men, flinched at the hand of one woman.

She came right up to him and touched him.

His body began to contract. Moisture, fluids emerged from every pore of his skin.

He dissolved away and I found myself, my thoughts spinning, in the middle of San Francisco

124

surrounded by so much firepower that they could have reduced me to shreds inside of five seconds.

It didn't matter to me.

Nothing mattered to me . . . because she was there.

My memory was fragmented, having experienced all that had happened through the distorted prism of the Hulk's perceptions. Still, despite my exhaustion, I was able to look up at Betty with bleary eyes and an exhausted half smile.

"You found me," I whispered hoarsely.

She looked around at the sea of guns aimed straight at me. "You weren't that hard to find," she said, noting the dark humor of the situation.

"Yes. I was."

She started to cry, and I held her tight. "I'm just grateful we got the chance . . . to say good-bye," I said to her.

That all happened earlier today.

Or yesterday. It's hard to be sure.

My hand is exhausted from writing it all down.

Most of it, as I'm sure you have figured out by now, I don't remember firsthand. Betty filled me in

125

on most of the gaps of my memory, which I've combined with my own patchy recollections.

At the moment, I'm sitting in a hangar at Joint Tactical Force West. They've put together a rather impressive little makeshift prison for me. I'm sitting on a chair, illuminated by large klieg lights, so I'm certainly having no trouble seeing. More to the point, my captors are having no trouble seeing me.

Lining the wall are huge electromagnetic arrays, ready to incinerate me at a moment's notice. If I start to turn even slightly green, I'll be a pile of dust long before I can transform into something tougher to stop.

Yet, with all that's happened, here's the most shocking thing of all:

Betty told me my father turned himself in.

He admitted everything to her. Everything he'd done. He's in military custody right now. She said he actually seems sorry, if such a creature can feel sorrow for anything. Apparently the only thing he asked is that he be allowed to see me one last time. Supposedly it's being arranged.

I don't know how to feel about that, or what to feel about him. Pity? Revulsion? Anger? Anger, I suppose, would make the most sense . . . but look where anger has gotten me. Where does anger get anyone, really, when you think about it?

I've no idea what they're going to do with me. But I do know one thing.

They can't afford to let me live.

I spent what I figured was going to be my last night on earth in fitful sleep. Images of my mother, stirred up from the deepest recesses of my memory, floated about, and I woke up repeatedly covered with sweat. Finally I couldn't sleep anymore. I had no idea whether it was night or day.

Then I heard footsteps approaching. A single pair. But too heavy to be Betty's. A man.

I stood up, and even though the bright lights were in my eyes, I recognized him instantly. My father . . . the mad scientist.

He walked the length of the hangar, in thick shackles. He stepped up onto the platform where I was being held and then just stood there. Apparently he was waiting for me to say something.

I thought of all the damage he had done. Of his murderous assault on my mother. Of him sending those hideous dogs after Betty. Not to mention everything he had done to me.

"I should have killed you," I told him.

"As I should have killed you," he replied.

I suppose families don't get much more dysfunctional than that.

"I wish you had," I said, and sank down onto the chair. "I saw her last night. In my mind's eye. I saw her face. Brown hair, brown eyes. She smiled at me. She leaned down and kissed my cheek. I can almost remember a smell, like desert flowers . . ."

He smiled. "Her favorite perfume," he said.

We were almost like two friends reminiscing about a lost love.

"My mother," I said with a sigh. "I don't even know her name."

My eyes started to moisten.

129

"Crying will do you good," he said softly, and started to reach toward me.

I flinched, told him to keep away. Once, perhaps, he'd been my father, but now he never would be nor could be, and I told him that.

That didn't appear to bother him. "I have news for you," he said. "I didn't come here to see you. I came for my son."

I was completely bewildered by the comment. His son? Was he now saying, despite all that had happened, all he'd said . . . that I wasn't his son?

He saw my confusion, and his face twisted in contempt. "My real son," he continued. "The one inside of you."

I knew then what he meant. He considered the Hulk, a creature born of rage and nursed with fury, to be his true flesh and blood. I saw the burning anger in David Banner's eyes and realized he was probably right. He was much closer in spirit to the Hulk than to me.

"Think whatever you like. I don't care. Just go now," I said.

David Banner laughed and whispered, "But

130

Bruce, I have found a cure . . . for me. You see, my cells too can transform. Absorb enormous amounts of energy. But, unlike your cells, mine are unstable." He leaned forward, speaking faster and with more urgency. "Bruce, I need your strength. I gave you life. Now you must give it back to me—only a million times more radiant, more powerful."

I told him to stop.

He didn't. He spoke of the things we could do to the army, to anyone who had ever harmed us or tried to hurt us. "We can make them and their flags and anthems and governments disappear in a flash. You . . . in me."

He was completely obsessed with power. He was actually insane enough to see the curse I lived under as some sort of blessing. Something that he could take advantage of.

I told him I'd rather die.

He said I would, indeed, die . . . and be reborn, greater than ever before, as part of him.

I'd had more than enough. I leaped to my feet and screamed, "*Go!*"

"I'll go!" he snarled back at me. Suddenly he

grabbed one of the thick electrical cables lining the floor and tore it apart. "Just watch me go." The live wires sputtered . . .

I couldn't believe it. It wasn't possible. The voltage should have killed him instantly.

Instead the electricity surged through him. I tried to leap toward him but I was bounced back by the current.

I heard the electromagnetic arrays flare to life and realized that General Ross had pulled the trigger. He didn't know what was happening with my father, nor did he know what was going to happen to me. So he was taking no chances.

He was going to incinerate the both of us, right then and there.

A good plan, in theory.

It didn't work.

Instead of destroying us, all the energy from the arrays flowed directly into the outstretched arms of my father. He absorbed it all, and laughed uproariously, as if it were the funniest thing in the world.

And then I realized. It was true, the rumors I'd heard. He'd gone to my lab, exposed himself to the nanomeds and gamma radiation to try to duplicate what had happened to me.

But the gamma rays didn't affect him in the same way.

The electrical energy flowed through his body, and he used it to crack apart and break open his shackles. His hands were free, and the arrays exploded in a blinding flash.

The entire hangar went dark.

My father laughed again and started toward me . . . except I wasn't there.

Instead a huge green fist slammed upward and into him.

It was the Hulk's fist that did it, but my own mind was far closer to awareness than it had been before. Because I . . . he . . . *we* were so focused on our common enemy—the man who had done this to us, the man who had stabbed our mother as she fought to protect us—that for the first time we were joined in our fury.

The punch from the Hulk sent my father hurtling upward, tearing through the roof of the hangar, up and across the bay. The Hulk, with a roar, leaped after him.

Get him! Get him! My voice sounded in the Hulk's head, directing his rage.

My father crashed to the ground near a mountain lake and, as he staggered to his feet, electricity crackling around him, the Hulk landed nearby. A full moon hung in the night sky over us as the Hulk pounded unceasingly on my father.

All the rage over what he had done to us, all the frustrations we'd known in our life, was focused into the two unstoppable objects that were the Hulk's fists.

He pounded on our father with enough force to shatter a mountain.

It didn't slow David Banner down.

From within the recesses of the Hulk's mind, I watched in astonishment as our father withstood each blow and, as he did so, seemed to grow bigger, greener. It was as if he was absorbing the energy, taking it into his own body.

The Hulk took a step back, realizing on some basic level that he was making his own enemy stronger. David Banner had become as big as the Hulk, and he seemed to want only more.

Falling back, the Hulk scooped up an enormous boulder, lifted it, and crashed it down on our father.

The impact caused David Banner to transform into stone, and then, seconds later, the Hulk pounded him into a small mountain of dust and rock fragments.

But that wasn't the end of it. Not at all.

Instead our father re-formed, sneering at us, laughing. The Hulk, propelled by white-hot fury, lashed out once again with his fists. Locked in struggle, pounding away at each other, their battle carried them to the water's edge.

With each blow, the air seemed to grow colder, vacant. Even the water started to turn icy.

I realized what was happening. The conversion of energy into matter was drawing the heat from all around us. The air was powering the continued transformations we were both undergoing. But there was nothing I could do about it. I might have been more aware than ever before of what was happening, but I was as helpless as ever to have any effect.

We were atop the lake, frozen solid underneath us, locked in a death struggle with our father. Layer upon layer of ice had formed, and our minds—the Hulk's and mine—were overlapping. For the first time, we were truly one, and thousands of images,

135

bits of memory and desire, suddenly came together into a moment of absolute calm.

We saw ourselves back in the desert, in our home, years ago, and David Banner was seated on the floor opposite us, smiling and laughing and playing with us as if we were all one big normal, happy family. We were waving the dolls around.

"This one can fly. He's faster," we said.

"But mine will eat yours right up," replied our father.

Panic flickered through our mind. "No! He won't!" we said. "Mine is flying away!"

"Yes, you're flying away," said our father, and he threw the doll down.

And suddenly my mind was back in the present, back facing my father, even though it was the Hulk's hands on him.

And I saw him for what he was.

Not a monster. But a man. A pathetic, horribly flawed man, but a man nevertheless. A man who had destroyed my life, my mother's life . . . and his own as well. And the true tragedy was that he'd had a son and wife who had loved him, and he'd been too insane to appreciate it.

I felt sorry for him. I pitied him.

I knew then how he was planning on winning. He was going to harness my rage, take it from me.

But he wasn't going to be able to.

Because I was going to take it from myself.

By forgiving him.

The Hulk shoved our fist against our father's stomach, and all our power flowed into him.

He didn't understand what was happening. He didn't understand that the Hulk's rage not only fueled him, but also contained him, shaped him into what he was.

Without that rage, there was nothing to hold him back, and all the power of the Hulk flowed into him all at once. The ice beneath us began to crack.

David Banner grew and grew, larger and larger, until he was towering over mountains. He should have been all-powerful, unstoppable.

But it was too much, too fast. It was like trying to use a paper cup to catch a tidal wave. The energy overflowed, tearing David Banner apart, the swirling energy building more and more.

And me?

The Hulk gone, I dropped through the melting ice

137

into the lake, fighting to survive, certain I was going to drown. . . .

Suddenly there was a white blast of light and sound and thunder, and I fell away into darkness.

It's been so long. So long since I made an entry in my diary.

They think I'm dead, of course.

How could they not?

After all, the army dropped a huge bomb on my father just as he was unable to keep or control any of the energy that was shredding his body.

No one could survive that. No one.

Well . . . one person could. A person who was at the bottom of a frozen lake when it happened. A person whose body was able to absorb the high levels of radiation unleashed by such a weapon and use it to power the cells of his body.

A person who the world thinks is dead.

I miss Betty, of course. I think about her all the time. But I don't dare write to her or get in touch with her. They're probably watching her, monitoring her mail, her phone lines. Best that I stay away.

For now, at least.

An interesting thing happened to me today, down here in South America. I'm working with the volunteers, helping distribute medicine to poor people who are trying to survive in this war-torn country. I have a thick beard and another name. No one knows me. I work with a lovely young woman named Marlo. She's sweet, but she's no Betty.

So today, while we were doing our jobs, several armed men showed up. Paramilitary types working for the government, if you can call the corrupt organization that runs this country a government.

They tried to take the medical supplies we were distributing. "These people are helping our enemies," the largest and nastiest of the gun-toting men said. "And maybe so are you."

One of them pushed a child out of the way to get

to the supplies, and I stepped in between them. "You shouldn't have done that. Now say you're sorry and get out of here."

They looked me up and down. They saw I was unarmed, saw I looked like nothing special.

I felt I should warn them.

So I did.

"You're making me angry," I said with a tight smile. "You wouldn't like me when I'm angry."

I was right. They didn't.

But me . . . I liked it just fine.

Look for these other books featuring the Hulk: